Destiny's
COURAGE

Look for these and other books about Linelle Destiny in the Linelle Destiny Series:

Visit www.thesecretsistersclub.com

Linelle Destiny Series

Destiny's
COURAGE

Dr. Alicia Holland
Illustrations by Anoop PC

Acknowledgements

I want to first honor God for placing in my heart to share my story with others. It was He whom brought Karen and I together to manifest this project. I am so grateful for Karen Hendry as she took my notes and helped write this fictitious book. There are truly no words to express my gratitude as you are truly a blessing.

I also want to thank Surendra Gupta for his creativity in formatting and Anoop PC for his creativity in bringing life to the designs and illustrations in this book series. Both of you are amazing!

Dedication

I dedicate this book series to my beautiful and talented daughters, Georgia and Amaiya Johnson. Remember, you are valued, loved, and competent. You are worthy!

Part 1
After Graduation

Chapter 1
Future Plans

Destiny is sitting on the sofa, looking at the brand new degree she is holding in her hands. Pride fills her whole being as she reads it over and over again. She did it! She is officially a teacher!

Michelle comes into the living room from the kitchen. "Hey, squirt," she says. "Hard to put it down, isn't it?"

"It sure is," Destiny replies. "I just can't believe I'm finally a teacher."

"You sure are and I am super proud of you." Michelle says this to Destiny, but really, Destiny is the one who is proud of her big sister.

Michelle has been a complete inspiration to Destiny. They had gone to college together and were in some of the same classes, but while Michelle started earlier than Destiny and went part-time, she managed to get her degree a semester before Destiny, all while taking care of a family and a new baby.

"So what now?" asks Michelle.

"I guess I look for a teaching job," Destiny says. "I can check with the Shenikah School. Since I did my student teaching there, they already know me, so maybe I can work for them."

Michelle nods her agreement. "That's as good a place to start as any."

Momma comes into the living room and says, "What are you all waggin' your chins about?"

"I was just telling Destiny how proud I am of her and asking her what she plans to do next," says Michelle.

"Pop and I are right proud of you, too, Destiny," says Momma. "You got any plans made in that smart head of yours?"

"Hoping Shenikah School might have something for me," Destiny answers.

"Well, I'm sure you'll find something close to home."

Michelle nods again. "Momma's right. Something will turn up."

"I know," says Destiny. She hopes so because she wants to find a good job and she wants to stay close to home.

The next morning, the phone rings while Destiny is looking for the phone number for Shenikah School. She answers the phone and it's the principal of the Shenikah School.

"May I speak to Destiny Sycamores, please?"

"This is Destiny," Destiny replies.

"Hi, Destiny. This is Derek Underhand, principal at Shenikah School. I understand you have graduated with your teaching degree and I am calling to offer you a substitute teaching position at our school."

"Oh, thank you!"

"Now, this is just a part-time position, on an as-needed basis, but it *is* permanent."

Destiny is bouncing up and down on the spot. "Yes, I understand. Thank you." Then Destiny remembers her professionalism. "I am pleased to accept your offer."

"Wonderful," says Principal Underhand. "What is a good day for you to come in and fill out the paperwork?"

"How about tomorrow morning at 9:00?" asks Destiny.

"That will be fine, Destiny. I look forward to seeing you then. Goodbye."

"Thanks again and goodbye." Destiny hangs up the phone and squeals with delight.

"What's all that racket?" calls Momma from the kitchen.

"I got a job, Momma," Destiny yells, running into the kitchen and hugging Momma. "I got a teaching job! A real teaching job!"

"That's wonderful, child, but it's no reason to go givin' your old Momma a heart attack."

"I know, Momma. I'm sorry. "I have to go to work now. I'll be back tonight."

"Bye, sugar," says Momma.

Destiny grabs her keys and hurries out the door.

Destiny arrives at the jewelry store a little early for her shift so she can talk with her manager about her schedule. She really hopes it won't be a problem to work her schedule around her teaching job because she would hate to give up her job at the jewelry store. It's a wonderful job.

"Mr. Milestone?" says Destiny. "I wanted to talk with you about my schedule."

"Sure, Destiny," says Mr. Milestone. "What's up?"

"Well," Destiny begins, "You know I graduated." Mr. Milestone nods and Destiny continues. "I got a call this morning from a school and I was offered a job, but it's only part-time. It's substitute teaching."

"I see," says Mr. Milestone.

"The thing is I really want to keep working here. I love this job and I'm hoping we can accommodate my teaching in the schedule. I'm not sure how often or how much notice I'll get when I'm called in, but I am definitely available evenings and weekends."

Mr. Milestone smiles. "Don't worry, Destiny. We'll work it out. You're our best worker and I wouldn't dream of letting you get away."

Destiny sighs with relief. "Thank you, Mr. Milestone. I really appreciate it."

Destiny puts her things in the back and gets ready to start her shift.

That night, Destiny has a dream that she has opened a tutoring center. It's quite large and she can see dozens of students working away. One, a girl about 12 years of age, comes up to her to ask her a math question.

Destiny wakes up. She is amazed at how natural she felt at the tutoring center. She is quite certain it's the right thing to do, but now is definitely not the right time. Destiny knows she's already pushing it in terms of commitments. She couldn't possible add another one right now. But she knows one day she will open a tutoring center. One day.

Morning has yet to lighten the sky, so Destiny rolls over and goes back to sleep.

Chapter 2
The Letter

Destiny walks into the school. The students haven't arrived yet, so the hallways are quiet. She goes into the office and the secretary is just hanging up the phone.

"Good morning, Mrs. Martinez," says Destiny as she checks her mailbox. It's nice to have her own mailbox, now that she's on staff at the school.

"Oh, honey, call me Phoebe," she says. "And good morning to you, too. It's nice to have you back."

"It's nice to be back."

"You can go on up and get ready, dear," says Phoebe. "It's good you left yourself some time to get organized."

"Thanks," says Destiny.

In the classroom, Destiny settles at the desk and in the center of it is the lesson plan for the day. All of a sudden, Destiny realizes she is on her own, that she doesn't have a teacher in the room who is in charge, like when she was a student teacher. She *is* the teacher in charge today and little butterflies start fluttering around in her stomach.

Then Destiny gets a hold of herself. *Just treat it like a tutoring session. You've worked with kids loads of times before.* With that, she settles in and gets ready for her day.

When the students arrive, Destiny welcomes them, introduces herself, and dives into the lesson. Once she starts teaching, everything feels completely natural. They are grade seven students and she is teaching them a Memorial Project called "Town Geometry."

Destiny realizes soon after starting the lesson that none of the students had ever seen geometry done in this way. This makes teaching the lesson even more fun, because Destiny is starting from scratch with these kids.

One student, Fiona, bases her project on Candy. She raises her hand and Destiny goes over to her. "Miss Sycamores, I am not quite sure how to approach this."

Destiny spends some time talking with Fiona, prompting her to come up with the answers herself. By the end of the class, Fiona is well on her way. It is a fantastic day!

As Destiny comes in the door after her teaching day, Momma calls from the kitchen, "Hello, sugar. A letter came for you today."

"Thanks, Momma!" Destiny finds the letter on the stand by the front door. It's from the State of Louisiana. *Hmmm,* Destiny thinks. She goes into the living room, sits on the sofa, and opens the letter.

After reading the letter, Destiny says, "Huh," to herself and goes into the kitchen.

"Momma, the letter was from the state. They say I have more money left from my scholarships."

"Well, child," says Momma, "I guess that's a good thing. Never hurts to have more money. What you gonna do with it?"

"I don't know," replies Destiny. "I don't imagine I can just take the money, but I could go back to school."

"What would you do in school? You're already trained to be a teacher."

"I have been thinking about doing my Master's degree," says Destiny. "I could do that."

"Well, you will be the most educated person in our family, if you do honey. Getting better education is a good thing. But are you sure you have time for that?"

"I'll make time," says Destiny. "It would really help my career if I did this, Momma. I could focus on an area of education that I am really interested in."

"OK, honey. I guess you know best."

Destiny kisses Momma on the cheek. "I'll put this away and then I'll be in to help with dinner."

Momma chuckles and shakes her head as Destiny races out of the kitchen.

A week later, Destiny has an appointment at the college to meet with Dr. Michelle Gino about doing her Master's degree. She finds the appropriate building and goes in, up to the second floor, and finds room 217. Destiny knocks on the door.

"Come in," calls a woman's voice.

Destiny walks in and Dr. Gino is sitting at her desk.

"Hello, Destiny." Dr. Gino stands up and extends her hand.

Destiny shakes Dr. Gino's hand and responds, "Hi, Dr. Gino. It's nice to meet you."

"Likewise, Destiny." Dr. Gino gestures to one of the chairs across from her and Destiny takes a seat. Dr. Gino sits, as well. "I've been looking over your transcript and experience. Very impressive."

"Thank you," says Destiny.

"And now you're thinking of doing a Master's degree?"

"Yes, mam."

"And you have come to me because...?"

Destiny is beginning to get nervous, like maybe she is making a mistake. But no, she really wants this. "Because you work in early childhood education and I would also like to focus on that area of education."

"I see," says Dr. Gino. "Have you thought about a thesis topic, yet?"

"I've given it some thought," says Destiny. "I was thinking of something to do with minority students."

Dr. Gino is silent for what seems like an eternity, considering what Destiny said. "Destiny," she finally says, "I would very much like to work with you."

Destiny sighs with relief.

"I have been considering an area of research that I think would be perfect for you, given your background. What do you think of taking a look at the emotional effects of the U.S. education system in Hispanic students? I think this is an area you would find very intriguing."

"That sounds wonderful, Dr. Gino," says Destiny.

"Well, that's settled, then," say Dr. Gino. "I'll fill out the necessary paperwork on my end and you can go ahead and register. We'll meet again next week to plan your approach to the research and thesis."

"Thank you so much, Dr. Gino!" says Destiny as she stands up. "I'll go start the registration process right now, before I go to work."

"That sounds fine, Destiny," says Dr. Gino. "And thank *you*. I believe you will make an excellent addition to my department."

Destiny says her goodbyes and leaves Dr. Gino's office happier than she has ever been. She makes her way to the registrar's office, hoping it won't take too long because she really wants to get herself registered and she has to be at work in an hour.

Chapter 3
Family Pride

Destiny is home in time for dinner later that day. After registering for her Master's degree she went to work at the jewelry store, where her work shift was quiet. Now she is sitting having a nice dinner with her family. Michelle has joined them tonight.

Destiny is hungry and the meatloaf seems to taste extra good tonight, but it could be that Destiny is just so happy. Everything seems to be falling into place just the way she wants it to.

"Did you get registered today, squirt?" asks Michelle, once the family is settled at the table.

"I sure did," answers Destiny. "I'll be working with Dr. Gino on minority children and how they are affected by our education system. I don't know the details, yet, but it sounds like it will be fascinating research."

"Destiny, we are right proud of you," says Pop.

"Sure are," says Momma.

"Yeah, me too. I won't be able to catch you now, though," says Michelle. "I won't have time for a Master's degree. I'll be too busy with my new job."

Everyone looks at Michelle, the astonishment showing on their faces.

"Yes," Michelle says, a big smile on her face, "I got a new job!"

"You already have a job," says Momma.

"I know, Momma, but this one is with the state. I'll be an analyst with them."

"That's great, honey," says Pop. "We didn't even know you were applying."

"I know," Michelle replies. "I didn't want to tell anyone until I got the job. No point in getting everyone's hopes up for no reason. Even Junior didn't know until yesterday, when I found out I got it. He's pretty happy."

"I bet he is. It'll get you out of the supermarket store. Pays better than that? Good benefits?"

"Yes, Pop," Michelle answers. "It pays much better. Paid vacation and sick leave. Health insurance and Pension. It'll seem like a dream."

"That's good," Pop says. "A good, secure future in a job like that."

"Both our girls are gonna be just fine," says Momma. "Of course, I knew they would be. They're smart ones, they are."

"Yes we will be fine, Momma," says Destiny, getting up and giving Momma a kiss on the cheek. "Michelle and I will clean up. Momma and Pop, you go relax."

"Thank you, girls," says Momma and she and Pop head for the living room. A few seconds later, Destiny can hear the voice of the newscaster on the evening news.

Later that evening, Destiny is in her room. She is supposed to be going over a lesson she is teaching the next day, but she's just sitting at her desk, daydreaming. Then a vision comes to her.

Destiny sees herself writing and writing and writing. She sees the words on the page. She is writing a book about tutoring. Chapter after chapter is written until she has a completed manuscript. She finds a publisher and her book is published.

Then Destiny sees herself in different countries around the world, promoting her book. She is in London, Paris, Amsterdam, Beijing. She can see herself in lecture halls, speaking in front of hundreds of people, talking about tutoring, its importance, and various methods to best help kids learn.

Then the vision is gone and Destiny is sitting at her desk, her open book in front of her, her pen in her hand. *Tutoring again,* she thinks. But not a tutoring center this time. Instead it's a book about tutoring.

Regardless of how she goes about it, it's clear to Destiny that tutoring is something that is meant to be in her life. She is meant to help kids and not just local kids, but kids around the world. The whole concept is very exciting and ideas begin to swirl around in Destiny's head.

Then Destiny shakes her head. Yes, tutoring will be in her life, but not right now. She is just about to begin her Master's degree and she is just starting her teaching career. She really needs to focus on those things first. Then, once she has more experience under her belt, she can branch out and look at how to help more kids than just the ones in her classroom.

Still, it takes Destiny a long time to focus and get through her lesson. Then it takes an even longer time for her go to sleep that night because she keeps imagining what her life will be like in the future. Destiny can barely contain her excitement, but she finally drifts off to sleep.

Part 2
Master's Program

Chapter 4
Juggling

Destiny knocks on Dr. Gino's office door. Dr. Gino is on the phone, but motions for Destiny to come in and take a seat at the table in the corner of her office. It's a round work table with three chairs. There is a big plant in the corner near the table.

Destiny sits down and can see out the window. The dark rain clouds are hovering overhead outside, the rain coming down in sheets. She left her wet umbrella outside Dr. Gino's office.

There is some material related to Destiny's thesis topic sitting on the table. Destiny feels like it's beckoning to her, enticing her to jump in and get started. She strains her neck to try to take a peak.

"All right, I'll do that," says Dr. Gino to whoever she is talking to on the phone. "Yes, thank you. Goodbye."

She hangs up the phone and types a few things into her computer. Then she joins Destiny at the table. "Sorry about that. Just something to do with some grant money I'm trying to get."

"That's okay," says Destiny. "I didn't mind waiting."

"Now, Destiny," says Dr. Gino. "I have gathered some initial material for you to start going through. There are a number of journal articles and you can use the references in those to find more. You'll need to conduct a complete literature review so you know where you are starting when it comes to your research and you need to be familiar with the work has been done before."

She pushes a stack of paper over to Destiny.

"There will also be some early childhood education classes you will be taking. These are all online classes and I have the login information for you here." She puts a single piece of paper on top of the pile of papers. "While you are working on these, we will narrow down the thesis research options and decide on a specific topic."

"Okay, thank you," Destiny says. She pulls the stack toward her and begins looking at the login information. More classes.

Dr. Gino stands up and brushes her pants off, as if there is invisible dust on them. "I hate to rush you, Destiny, but I have a meeting to go to. But please call or email me if you have any questions."

"I will," says Destiny, standing up. She grabs the papers and puts them into her bag. "Thanks so much. Goodbye."

"Bye, Destiny."

Destiny walks out of Dr. Gino's office, grabs her umbrella, and heads down the hall, thinking about what awaits her. She is worried she won't have the time for all of these classes and extra work, but no, she'll make the time. Somehow.

Destiny is sitting at the kitchen table with her head in her hands, looking at the list of classes in front of her. At least everything is online so she can organize it all around her various jobs. That's way better that having specific class times to show up for on campus. If she had physical classes to go to, Destiny doubts she could pull this off.

She sighs.

"What's all that sighin' for, child?" Momma walks into the kitchen.

"Oh, nothing, Momma," says Destiny. "Just wrapping my head around all this work that needs to be done and trying figure out when I can get my class work done."

"More classes?" says Momma.

"That's what I said to myself today when I found out."

Momma looks over Destiny's shoulder. "That's quite a list. How are you gonna have time for all that?"

"Well, I have a couple of evenings free during the week and I generally have at least one day on the weekends, so I'll manage. The courses are all online, so I don't have to go to a classroom at a certain time each week."

Momma starts taking dishes out of the cupboard and sets to making dinner. "Well, sugar, just don't you go overdoin' it now, you hear? You need time for relaxin' and hangin' out with friends. You barely do that now."

"I know, Momma. I'll figure it out and I promise I'll make time for fun."

"Good," says Momma. "Right now I want you to make time to help make dinner."

Destiny chuckles. "Sure, Momma. Just let me put these things away."

That evening, alone in her room, Destiny thinks about her conversation with Momma. She has no idea how she will find enough time to keep up with her studies and everything else, let alone have time for friends.

Well, maybe that's fine. She doesn't have a lot of people she wants to hang out with anyway. Josephine moved back up north with her husband. The rest of her friends aren't interested in anything more than hanging out and spreading gossip. They have no greater goals in life. Plus, Destiny doesn't have a boyfriend right now, which means she doesn't have to try to find time to fit a man into her life.

Destiny knows she has a bright future ahead of her with so many things she is meant to achieve. Some sacrifice now will be worthwhile if it means making her future a success and she isn't going to be held back by a few scheduling issues.

Destiny spends the next half hour working out her schedule. When she is done, she leans back in her chair and looks at the final results. It's definitely something she can live with. Destiny knows she will manage and everything will work out just fine.

Chapter 5
Anderson

Destiny grabs her purse and walks out of the jewelry store. The mall is packed full of busy shoppers and Destiny is happy it is so close to Christmas and not just because it's Christmas, which is always a nice time of year all on its own.

Destiny has always loved Christmas because it feels so magical, so warm and full of love. But this year, Destiny loves it even more because it means she gets to slow down. She has been so busy with teaching, tutoring, and her online course-work that she has barely had time to breathe. Up at dawn – before dawn some days – and going until her head hits the pillow late each night.

With the holidays arriving, the most Destiny has to do is work some extra hours at the jewelry store and visit with family. The holidays are even more special than they usually are because Destiny will appreciate the peace and quiet more than she ever has before.

As Destiny walks into the food court, she begins to think about what she feels like eating for dinner. Maybe Chinese tonight? Or a sub? Yes a sub. Just as she turns toward the sub shop, she hears someone shout out, "Hey, Destiny!"

She turns and there is a young man about her age. She takes a closer look and realizes it's Anderson Watson. She went to high school with him. High school seems like it was so long ago. So much has changed since then.

Destiny walks over to where Anderson has a small sound system set up in front of the music store next to the food court. "Hi, Anderson," she says.

"Long time no see, Destiny," says Anderson. "You work here in the mall?"

Destiny nods. "Yeah, I work at the jewelry store. Have done for a couple of years."

"Cool. What else are you up to?"

"Well," says Destiny. "I'm a teacher now. Just subbing right now, until something full-time opens up, but working with kids and loving it. Getting my Master's degree, too. What about you?"

"That's awesome, Destiny. Although, I'm not surprised. You always had it in you to do big things." Destiny can feel her cheeks flushing a little. "As for me, I'm all into the music scene right now. Hey, listen to this."

Anderson plays some music for Destiny. His body is moving to the beat, eyes closed, totally into it. Destiny likes it. It sounds soulful, but has a good rhythm to it. It would be good to dance to.

"You like it?" asks Anderson.

"I do," says Destiny, feeling the music. "Listen, Anderson, I hate to run, but I need to get some dinner before my break is up. It's been nice chatting with you, though."

"You, too, Destiny. Hey, maybe we could go out some time. Tomorrow?"

The request shocks Destiny. Anderson never paid much attention to her in high school, at least not in a dating sort of way. But she is intrigued. He is very good looking and she always thought so, even in high school.

"I'd like that," Destiny says. She gives Anderson her phone number and they make plans to see each other the following evening after Destiny gets off work.

Destiny goes and gets her sub and heads back to the jewelry store to eat it in the staff room. It amazes her how finding a date can seemingly come out of nowhere, when it is least expected. But she is on cloud nine and very excited about her date with Anderson.

When Destiny gets off work the next day, she is closing the jewelry store. She pulls the door of the store shut and locks it. Then she walks to the bank and makes her deposit. The last of the shoppers are leaving the various stores and the mall is emptier than she has seen it all day. The clicking sound of her shoes hitting the floor echo through the nearly empty hallways.

Destiny meets Anderson by the mall exit. They had talked on the phone that morning and made plans to meet up and have dinner at the diner downtown. They take Destiny's car and drive to the diner, making small talk about their day and how busy the mall was while they drive.

"Are you ready for Christmas?" asks Destiny, as she parks the car. She lucks out and gets a spot right in front of the diner.

As they get out of the car and shut their doors, Anderson says, "No, not really. Have a few gifts bought but nothing much yet. You?"

"Most of my shopping is done," says Destiny as Anderson holds the door of the diner open for her.

"Somehow that doesn't surprise me," says Anderson.

They find an empty booth. "Why not?" asks Destiny.

"Well, you're always so organized. I can't imagine you not being prepared for anything and I definitely can't imagine you leaving *anything* to the last minute."

"Haha," says Destiny. "I guess I never really thought about it. I just like to be prepared. I don't like the feeling I get when I'm not."

The waitress comes by and they order, Anderson a hamburger combo and Destiny and club sandwich. The waitress, her name tag says she is Jennifer, fills their water glasses and leaves.

"So a Master's degree, huh?"

"Yeah, in early childhood education."

"Plus teaching part-time and working at the jewelry store? You're one busy woman."

"And tutoring part-time."

"OK, wow. I would say your superwoman."

"I don't know about that," says Destiny. "What about you? What are your plans for the future?"

"Music and medicine," says Anderson.

"Care to elaborate?"

"Well, right now a friend of mine and I are working on starting a record label. It's called Glimira Records. That's more short-term, though. In the long-term, I plan on moving to Texas and going into sports medicine."

"You sound like you're pretty busy, yourself," says Destiny. "You definitely will be when you start your medical degree."

"Don't I know it," says Anderson.

Their meals come and the two talk as they eat. Destiny finds it so easy to talk to Anderson. She feels at ease with him and it feels nice.

After their date, Anderson says he'll walk home and so they say goodbye. Anderson gives Destiny a kiss on the cheek and Destiny feels wonderful as she drives home. When she parks her car and goes in, the lights are all off. Her parents must have gone to bed early, so Destiny is quiet as she slips off her shoes and coat and heads to her room.

Once in her room and ready for bed, Destiny sits at her desk and thinks about Anderson. She never would have guessed back in high school that she would one day date him. And he is so different from the guys she has gone out with. He is so creative musically and so talented. This will surely be a good thing. Fitting dating into her already busy schedule will be a challenge, but Anderson is worth it. Besides, she doesn't really have to worry about time too much until after the holidays are over.

Destiny sighs and grabs a book to read before bed. Life really is good.

Chapter 6
Land

The holidays are over and Destiny has gotten into the swing of things over the winter, including having a boy-friend. She has no idea how she has found the time to fit in dates and time with Anderson, but he is really understanding when it comes to her schedule. Plus, Anderson is very busy with his music, so he keeps himself occupied when he's not with Destiny.

Spring has finally arrived, bringing with it the promise of warm summer days. One evening, Michelle is visiting and she and Destiny are sitting on the front porch, chatting over a cup of tea.

"So, sis," says Michelle. "How's Anderson?"

"He's fine, thanks," answers Destiny.

"He's a nice guy," says Michelle, the approval clear in her voice. "You should keep this one."

"We'll see."

"How is work?"

Destiny sips her tea and answers, "It's good. All of it."

"You must have some money saved up by now," says Michelle. "You're working three jobs and living at home."

"I do, actually," says Destiny, "and I've been trying to decide what to do with it. I want to do something smart, ya know?"

"I get it," says Michelle. "The smartest thing I know to do with your money is to somehow invest it in your future. Since you don't need to pay for your education, maybe you should find another way to invest that money. You know, make sure it keeps working for you?"

"I was thinking about buying a house. Do you think I have enough to do that?"

Michelle shakes her head. "You don't have steady full-time employment, so no bank is going to give you a mortgage, but you could buy some land, if you have enough money. You could probably get some land at a good price."

"I could do that," says Destiny. "Then, when I'm ready, I could build a house on it."

"Yup, that would be smart," says Michelle.

"I'll get in touch with a real estate agent tomorrow and find out my options."

"That's a good idea," says Michelle. "Now, it's getting mighty chilly out here. Time to go inside."

They take their tea inside and a little while later Michelle goes home to put her kids to bed.

The next day, Destiny goes into a real estate agent's office when she is done teaching for the day. When she goes in, the receptionist greets her. "Hi there. What can I do for you today?"

"Hello. My name is Destiny Sycamores and I would like to speak with an agent about purchasing some land."

"Well, sugar," says the woman, "why don't you take a seat and I'll let Mr. Biggs know you're here."

"Thank you." Destiny sits down in the waiting room. She barely flips open a magazine when a short, dark-haired man in a dark gray business suit comes out to meet her.

Destiny stands up and shakes the man's hand. "Hello there. Miss Sycamores, is it?"

Destiny nods, "Yes, Destiny Sycamores."

"I'm Mr. Biggs, Destiny. Come on into my office."

Destiny follows the man through a door on the far side of the receptionist's desk. Once inside, Mr. Biggs gestures to a chair for Destiny as he takes a seat at his desk.

"What can I do for you today, Miss Sycamores?"

"I have some money saved up and I am interested in purchasing some land. You know, something for the future."

Mr. Biggs nods his head thoughtfully. "I can see you're a smart lady, Miss Sycamores. Investing in land is a wise move. Where were you thinking of buying some property?"

"Well, I want to stay close to my parents. They are on Taylor Street."

"I think we have some properties in that area, Miss Sycamores. Why don't you give me 24 hours or so to look over what's available and get back to you?"

"That would be fine," says Destiny, standing up. "Thank you."

"Great," says Mr. Biggs. "You just leave your phone number with my receptionist and I'll call you as soon as I have some options."

Mr. Biggs walks Destiny out of his office and shakes her hand again. Destiny leaves her phone number with the receptionist and goes home to help with dinner. Momma is in the kitchen when she gets there.

"You're late today, sugar," says Momma.

Destiny decides not to tell her parents about the land purchase, not until it's official. "Oh, I stayed late to mark the tests I got back today. Sorry about that, Momma. I should have called."

"That's fine, honey. I know you are working hard."

They get dinner and Destiny sits down to eat with Momma and Pop. After dinner, Destiny is cleaning up when the phone rings. Destiny answers it. "Hello?"

"Miss Destiny Sycamores, please."

"This is Destiny."

"Ah, Miss Sycamores. It's Mr. Biggs. Do you have a moment?"

Destiny drapes the dish towel over her shoulder and sits down at the kitchen table. "Yes, I do," she replies.

"Wonderful," says Mr. Biggs. "I've found two properties that I think suit your needs very well. They are both relatively close to where your parents live."

"That's great, Mr. Biggs."

"Do you have time to take a look at them tomorrow?" asks Mr. Biggs.

"I can see them in the morning," Destiny replies. "How is 9:30?"

"That sounds fine. Why don't you meet me at my office and we'll go from there."

"I'll do that and thank you, Mr. Biggs."

"You're welcome, Miss Sycamores. Goodbye."

"Goodbye," says Destiny. She hangs up the phone.

"Who was callin'?" asks Momma from the living room.

"Oh, just Anderson," says Destiny in a white lie. Excitement builds in her as she finishes the dishes.

Destiny walks into the real estate office just as Mr. Biggs is coming out of his office. "Good morning, Miss Sycamores. I am glad to see you are prompt."

"Good morning, Mr. Biggs." The receptionist isn't at her desk, so Destiny figures she must be in the back room or running an errand.

"Follow me," says Mr. Biggs.

They go outside and to the parking lot and get into Mr. Biggs' Cadillac. Over the next hour they visit both sites. The one closer to her parents' house is lovely and it's a fairly large lot, but the one that is slightly further away is a dream. It's one and a half acres, which gives Destiny loads of space for a big house and a big yard and maybe even a swimming pool one day.

After they get back to the real estate office, Destiny tells Mr. Biggs she will think it over and get back to him later that day. "Don't wait too long, Miss Sycamores. Properties like those don't last long."

"I won't, Mr. Biggs. I'll let you know by this evening."

Destiny gets into her car and heads to the mall for her shift at the jewelry store. She thinks about the properties the entire time she's at work. She really likes the bigger one, but by the end of her shift she has decided on the one closer to her parents' home. It's just a few blocks away, within walking distance when the weather is decent.

When she gets home, Destiny calls Mr. Biggs. "Biggs here," he answers.

"Hello, Mr. Biggs. This is Destiny Sycamores."

"Hello, Miss Sycamores. I'm glad to hear from you."

"Yes," says Destiny. "Well, I've chosen the property on Louisiana Avenue."

"I'm sorry to say that property has been sold, Miss Sycamores," says Mr. Biggs. "I just found out, myself."

"Oh, okay," says Destiny. Oddly enough, she doesn't feel that disappointed. "Is the other one still available? The one on Buffalo Drive?"

"Why, yes it is," says Mr. Biggs, "and might I say that it is a lovely property. Nice and spacious."

"Yes, it is," says Destiny. "I will take that one then. I do really like it."

"That's a fine choice. When would you like to come in and finalize the deal?"

"I can come in Monday morning. I'll be paying cash, so I can bring a certified cheque, if that's okay."

"That would be just fine," says Mr. Biggs. "I'll see you then."

Destiny hangs up and realizes she is about to buy her own land. She feels amazed at what she has accomplished and realizes she truly is an adult. After all, adults buy land and invest their money in their future. Destiny skips out of the house to meet Anderson for a date at the movies.

Part 3
Decisions

Chapter 7
Hiring Freeze

Destiny is leaving a meeting with her thesis advisor, Dr. Gino. As she exits the building the spring air hits her and she feels wonderful. How can anyone not feel amazing when spring is in the air?

On her way down the steps, Destiny runs into Dr. Paul, who taught her Social Teaching Methods when she was doing her undergraduate program.

"Hello, Destiny," says Dr. Paul.

"Hi, Dr. Paul."

"How have you been?" he asks. "I hear you are substitute teaching now. At...?"

"Yes, at Shenikah School."

"Are you enjoying it?"

"Yes," says Destiny. "Very much. I'd really like to teach there full-time, but I've heard there is a hiring freeze in Louisiana right now, so I don't know when I'll get a permanent, full-time position."

"Yes," replies Dr. Paul, "They announced the hiring freeze just last month. You know, Destiny, there are great teaching opportunities in Texas. Have you ever thought about applying there?"

"Not really. I'd like to stay close to home, so I have only ever looked for jobs here."

"I understand the desire to stay close to home and close to family," says Dr. Paul, "but unfortunately sometimes our circumstances don't allow that." He reaches into his briefcase and pulls out a pen and a piece of paper. He writes something down and gives the paper to Destiny.

"This is a contact of mine in Texas," he says. "Give it some thought and if you think it might be a good move for you, then give her a call. I know you are a great teacher and you would be an asset to any school. Louisiana will be sorry to lose you, but you have to take care of yourself and your future."

"Thank you," says Destiny. "I will definitely think about it. I have to run now or I'll be late for my job at the jewelry store. Good bye, Dr. Paul."

"Good bye, Destiny, and good luck."

When Destiny reaches her car, she gets in and looks at the paper. Dr. Paul had written the name Dr. Patricia Applegate, along with her phone number. Destiny tucks the paper into her purse and starts her car, thinking she is not ready to leave home. Not yet, anyway.

Three days later, Destiny is listening to the news and hears a report on the hiring freeze in the state. It sounds like it might go on for a long time and she is concerned that she might not get a full-time teaching job for a very long time. Then Destiny remembers the contact Dr. Paul gave her.

Destiny goes out into the front hallway and reaches into her purse, which is hanging by the front door. She digs around a bit and pulls out the paper Dr. Paul had given her. It's a bit crumpled up, but easily readable. Destiny goes back into the kitchen and dials the number written on the paper.

"Hello," says a voice on the other end of the line. "Dr. Applegate speaking."

"Hi, Dr. Applegate," says Destiny, suddenly feeling nervous. "My name is Destiny Sycamores. Dr. Paul gave me your number and thought you might be able to help me find a teaching job in Texas."

"Yes, Destiny. I just spoke with Dr. Paul yesterday and he gave me a heads-up that you might call. He had some very good things to say about you."

"Thank you," says Destiny.

"I will be in your area in a couple of weeks," says Dr. Applegate. "Why don't you give me your phone number? When I get into town, I'll give you a call and we can set up a time to meet and talk about your prospects."

"That would be wonderful," says Destiny. She gives Dr. Applegate her number and says goodbye. Tingles shoot through her body as she hangs up. It's such a big decision, a big move. Excited, Destiny gets ready for her dinner date with Anderson.

Anderson has taken Destiny to a nice Italian restaurant for dinner. It's a little fancier than the usual dates they go on, but they have been seeing each other for six months now and he decided to celebrate.

"You look really nice tonight," says Anderson after they order dinner. They both order the same chicken pasta dish.

"Thanks," says Destiny. "So do you."

"So, your first year of teaching is almost done," says Anderson. "What will you do after that? I heard about the hiring freeze and I know that means you'll have a hard time finding a full-time job."

Destiny decided earlier in the day that she wasn't going to say anything to Anderson about the possibility of her getting a teaching job in Texas. After all, she doesn't even know if she will get the job and things are going so well with him that she doesn't want to rock the boat.

"Yeah, that's true," Destiny replies. "But the hiring freeze can't last forever."

"It sounds like it might last for a while," says Anderson. "Are you going to be okay with that?"

"I'll be fine. The school has told me that my substitute teaching position is permanent, so I know I have at least that, plus my job at the jewelry store and tutoring. It just means I might have to live at home for a while longer, that's all. Then when the hiring freeze is over, I'll get a full-time job and all will be well."

"You're sure?"

"Yes," says Destiny. "Besides, my Master's degree will keep me too busy for full-time teaching. The timing of this hiring freeze couldn't be better. Now stop worrying, Anderson."

Anderson smiles at Destiny. "Okay, okay. Just making sure."

"I know," says Destiny. They enjoy the rest of their dinner and the conversation shifts to Anderson's music, much to Destiny's relief.

Chapter 8
Discussion

It's almost eleven o'clock in the morning when the phone rings. Momma answers it in the living room and shouts, "Destiny, phone's for you!"

Destiny picks up the extension in the kitchen. "Hello," she says.

"Hi, Destiny. Dr. Applegate here."

Destiny had almost forgotten about Dr. Applegate and the interview she would be having. Well, forgot isn't really the right word. It's more like it had been pushed to the back of her mind because she has been so busy.

"Oh yes. Hi, Dr. Applegate," says Destiny.

"Hi, Destiny. I am in town. I know it's short notice, but if you can meet me at the college this afternoon, we can talk about a teaching position for you. How is one thirty?"

Destiny does a little happy dance on the spot. "One thirty is fine, Dr. Applegate. Where should I meet you?"

"Come to Dr. Paul's office."

"Wonderful," says Destiny. "I'll see you then."

They say their goodbyes and Destiny hangs up the phone. It's a good thing Destiny has her afternoon free, but she needs to get ready to go. She definitely doesn't want to be late for this meeting.

A few minutes later, Destiny comes out of her room with her backpack and purse. She sets them by the door and goes into the kitchen. Michelle is sitting at the table and Momma is puttering around getting lunch.

"I thought I heard you come in," Destiny says to Michelle.

"Yup," says Michelle. "I always love it when Momma feeds me."

"You a spoiled girl, you know that, Michelle?" says Momma. "Do you want a sandwich, Destiny?"

"No, thank you," says Destiny, filling her travel mug with coffee. "I have to go. I'll get something while I'm out."

"Who was on the phone earlier?" asks Momma.

"Bet it was Anderson," says Michelle. "You are still seeing him, right? Or was it some other boy fawning after you?"

"Yes, I'm still seeing Anderson and no it wasn't a guy on the phone." Destiny takes a deep breath. "Actually, I am going for an interview for a full-time teaching job."

"That's great," says Michelle. "Where will you be teaching?"

"That's the most exciting part," says Destiny. "It's in Texas!"

Michelle and Momma just stare at Destiny, then Michelle says, "Come again?"

"Well, there isn't any full-time work here right now, not with the hiring freeze. Dr. Paul, one of my undergrad professors at the college, put me in touch with a colleague of his in Texas and she has a job for me. I'm meeting her for an interview this afternoon."

"Well, now sugar," says Momma, "I know you need work, but moving so far away? I don't like it. Family needs to stay close, stick together." Michelle is nodding.

"At first I didn't want to do it, but it sounds like this hiring freeze is going to go on for a while and I need to find a permanent, full-time teaching position. There just aren't any here."

"Honey, I don't think that hiring freeze'll last that long," says Momma. "Besides, you can go on living here with me and Pop. You ain't got no expenses or rent here. A good roof over your head and your family around."

"She's right, squirt," says Michelle. "You can't move that far away. It just wouldn't be right."

Destiny sighs and looks at the clock on the wall. This discussion is going nowhere, and at this rate, neither is she.

"Listen, I have to go or I'll be late for my interview," says Destiny. "I know you guys have reservations about this, but we can talk more about it later. It's not like she's going to give me a job on the spot and have me sign papers."

"I do want to talk about this more," says Momma, "and Pop will have a few words to say about it, too." Michelle doesn't say anything, but Destiny doesn't like the look on her face.

"Okay, well, I have to go, now," says Destiny.

"Give me some sugar, honey," says Momma, and Destiny kisses her on the cheek. Then she runs out of the kitchen before anyone says anything else. She is almost out the door, when Michelle catches her.

"You know it'll kill Momma and Pop if you do this, if you move," says Michelle. She doesn't quite look angry. More sad and pleading.

Destiny just nods and rushes out the door before Michelle says anything else.

Destiny is only about five minutes from the college campus, but traffic is backed up a long way and has been crawling along for at least fifteen minutes. Frustration is building in her. What is taking so long?

She finally reaches a police officer who is directing traffic and rolls down her window. "Excuse me, officer," Destiny says. "What's happening?"

"There's been an accident," says the officer. "We're rerouting traffic down Aspen Street."

"Okay, thank you." Destiny closes her window and sighs, something she seems to be doing a lot today. She doesn't have time to wait in this traffic or to go the long way around, but there isn't anything she can do about it. She looks at her watch and it is two minutes to two. Not good.

Five minutes later, she is turning the corner at Aspen Street and traffic begins to move a little faster, but it's another ten minutes before she gets to the campus.

Destiny parks her car and runs as fast as she can to Dr. Paul's office. Up the stairs and down the hall she sprints, nearly out of breath. Just as she reaches Dr. Paul's office, a woman who she presumes in Dr. Applegate is coming out the door.

"Dr. Applegate," pants Destiny between breaths. "I'm so sorry I'm late. There was a car accident not far from here and it held me up. I was stuck in traffic for at least twenty minutes." Destiny doesn't add that she left her house later than she had planned because of the argument with her family about moving to Texas.

"Hi, Destiny," says Dr. Applegate. "I understand. Sometimes these things happen. But right now I have a meeting to get to, so I don't have time to meet with you. Can you come tomorrow morning? I can meet with you for a few minutes, then. Say at nine o'clock?"

Destiny nods, "Yes, I can be here. Thank you so much, Dr. Applegate."

"No problem, Destiny. I'll see you tomorrow." She turns and heads off down the hallway and Destiny leans against the wall to finish catching her breath and say a prayer of thanks for being given a second chance.

Destiny doesn't know why, but she just has a feeling this Texas teaching job is supposed to happen, even though it will mean leaving her family. Her decision seems so easy now. She will take the job if she gets it. The only real hard part will be convincing her family it's a good move.

Chapter 9
Interview

When nine o'clock the next morning arrives, Destiny is already standing outside Dr. Paul's office waiting for Dr. Applegate to arrive. There is no way she is going to be late again. But she left in plenty of time this morning and traffic flowed fairly smoothly, so she got there with ten minutes to spare.

When the office door opens, she expects Dr. Applegate to appear, but instead Dr. Paul comes out. "Oh, hi, Destiny," he says. "Dr. Applegate will be here in about five minutes."

"Oh, okay, thanks," says Destiny.

"Don't worry about it," he says, sensing her nervousness. "You'll do fine. You'd be an asset to any school. Plus, I put in a good word for you."

With that, Dr. Paul winks at Destiny and heads off down the hallway, leaving her with her nervousness. She got off on the wrong foot with Dr. Applegate yesterday and she hopes the interview goes smoothly today. Her whole future is counting on this interview.

Not long after Dr. Paul disappears down the hallway, Destiny can see Dr. Applegate coming toward her. She looks rushed.

"Good morning, Destiny," says Dr. Applegate. "It looks like I'm the one who needs to apologize for being late today. Have you been waiting long?"

"No, no," says Destiny. "Not long. It's no problem, Dr. Applegate."

"Thank you," replies Dr. Applegate. "This is what I get for packing too many things into a three-day visit."

Dr. Applegate opens the office door and the two of them go inside. There is a small, round table in the corner of the office and they each take a seat at it. Dr. Applegate puts her things down and takes off her light, magenta jacket, draping it on the chair behind her. Then she takes some papers out of her briefcase.

"So, Destiny," says Dr. Applegate. "Dr. Paul can't say enough good things about you."

Destiny can feel her cheeks getting warm. It seems Dr. Applegate notices. "Now, don't you be modest, Destiny," Dr. Applegate says in her Texas drawl. "You need to toot your own horn sometimes to get ahead in this world, especially as a woman."

Destiny nods and does her best to relax.

"What is your teaching experience, thus far," asks Dr. Applegate.

"I have spent the past school year as a substitute teacher with Shenikah School. They have said they would like to hire me full-time, but with the hiring freeze here in Louisiana, they can't."

"Now that's more like it," says Dr. Applegate. "What grades are you teaching there?"

"I've been teaching math to grades six, seven, and eight. I'm also starting my Master's degree in early childhood education and I'm currently taking some online courses toward that."

"I see," says Dr. Applegate, nodding. "Impressive. One final question. Are you okay with moving to Texas? Moving away from home isn't for everyone and I really need to ask because if I hire you, then you need to be committed to the move."

Destiny nods. "I know and I've given it a lot of thought. At first I wasn't sure, but now I am. Actually, I'm excited by the idea of it and very much looking forward to the opportunity. If I get the job, of course."

"Well, Destiny. I'm impressed. Very impressed. I would like to offer you a job teaching grade seven and eight math at CD Heights Middle School in Round Rock, Texas."

Destiny is stunned. She honestly didn't think this would happen so quickly. Surely there were other applicants.

As if she knows exactly what Destiny is thinking, Dr. Applegate says, "I know a good teacher when I see one, Destiny, and I don't like to let the good ones get away." She slides the papers she had taken out of her briefcase in front of Destiny. It's a contract and other government paperwork. "What do you think? Will you accept the position?"

Destiny finds her voice and says, "Yes! Absolutely, I will accept it, Dr. Applegate."

"Wonderful. If you can sign the contract and quickly fill out this paperwork, I will take everything with me and get the ball rolling in Texas. I will also need a copy of your transcript and a

reference letter from the principal at Shenikah School, but you can mail or fax those to me.

"That sounds, fine," says Destiny, as she starts writing. "I will get everything you need and send it to you."

"Fabulous! You'll also need to start making plans to move. I can send you some information on real estate and apartment rentals to help get you started."

"That would be great," says Destiny. "Thank you!"

"Perfect," says Dr. Applegate. While Destiny is filling out the paperwork, she pulls some other papers out of her briefcase and reads over them.

Nearly ten minutes later, Destiny finishes filling out the forms and hands them to Dr. Applegate. "All done," she says.

"Thank you, Destiny. Once again I have to run. I have one more meeting to attend before I head back home. Here is my business card. You can send everything to that address and call me if you have any questions. I look forward to hearing from you soon."

Dr. Applegate is already standing up and putting on her jacket. Destiny also stands and they leave the office, say their goodbyes, and part ways.

Once Destiny reaches her car, she gets in and sits for a while. The silence is calming, good for her nerves, which are on edge because she knows she will have to tell her family she is moving. She will also have to tell Anderson. She's not looking forward to that, either.

But despite her nervousness at telling her loved ones about the big move that is coming, Destiny still feels exhilarated.

After all, she is now a fully employed teacher. Plus, she is going on a new adventure, moving to a new place to experience new things. It's such a big step in her life, but she knows it's the right one. There is just something in her gut that tells her it is.

As she starts her car and drives out of the college parking lot, Destiny says a little prayer, asking for guidance on how to tell her family and Anderson that she is moving away. She can only hope that even though they will feel sad, they will be happy for her and support her decision.

Chapter 10
Epilogue

On the way home from her interview, Destiny thinks things through. She has two options. The first is to continue to work part-time as a teacher and in various other jobs to make ends meet and to keep living at home with her parents. The second is to get a real, permanent, full-time teaching position, which would require her to move, not only away from her parents' home, but out of state.

Destiny realizes how big of a decision this is. It will be a defining decision in her life, one she needs to take very seriously. The butterflies in her stomach cause her to pull off onto a side street and pull over for a moment.

Wow. And she has accepted the job. It's done. Is this really what she wants? Before the question is even finished running through her mind it is being chased by the obvious answer. Yes!

Now she just has to tell her family. The thought of that makes Destiny's insides clench up tight. But she knows she has to stand up to them all. It's time she started making her own decisions.

Destiny starts driving again. Better get this over with, she thinks.

Destiny takes a deep breath and opens the front door of her house. She can hear Michelle and Momma talking in the kitchen as she sets down her keys and bag.

It's now or never, Destiny thinks.

When she walks into the kitchen, Michelle and Momma stop talking and look up at her.

"It's done, ain't it?" asks Momma.

Destiny nods.

"Well, sit down child," says Momma. "Tell us about it."

Destiny sits across the table from Michelle, next to Momma. She folds her hands on the table in front of her and waits for someone other than her to start the conversation.

"Well?" says Michelle after a minute.

"I have the job," says Destiny. She doesn't know what else to say.

"I see," says Momma. "Is it a good job?"

"Yes," says Destiny.

"Are you happy about it?"

"Well, yes," says Destiny with hesitation.

"I'll tell ya I'm not, child," says Momma. Destiny cringes inside, waiting for the lecture, for Momma to say she can't go. "But I understand," finishes Momma.

Destiny doesn't know what to say. She just sits there in stunned silence.

"Well, aren't you going to say something?" says Michelle.

"Thank you," says Destiny.

Momma takes Destiny's hand. "I honestly wasn't sure what I was gonna say when you told me the news, honey. Lord knows I don't want my baby going so far away. But your Pop and I talked about it and we know you need a good future. If you have to move to get it, then that's the way it has to be."

Momma stands up and starts cleaning up the tea. "Nothing good in this life ever comes easy, child, and life doesn't always go the way we want it to." She turns and faces Destiny, tears streaming down her cheeks. "But we are a strong family, sugar, and we will get through this."

Destiny stands up and throws her arms around Momma. "Oh, thank you, Momma!"

"And you gonna come home every chance you get, you hear?"

"Oh, I will Momma. I will!"

The next thing Destiny knows, Michelle is hugging her and Momma and the three of them are crying, all together.

Later that evening, Destiny is in her room thinking about everything she has to do. She has to find a place to live in Austin, set up her phone and utilities, pack, hire a truck. So much!

It's overwhelming. But then Destiny realizes that her whole life is about to change and it will never, ever be the same again. She is all grown up, now. A new job, students of her own, her own apartment, and a date with Alvin once she gets there in Austin.

Destiny has a big move ahead of her!

About the Author

Alicia Linelle Holland was born and raised in Many, Louisiana and got her middle name after her mother, Vera Linelle. When Alicia was in middle school, she started the Secret Sister Club that you read about in the Linelle Destiny Book Series. Alicia Holland has been working towards bringing back the Secret Sister Club as she embarks upon quite an interesting life and spiritual journey. At age 26, she earned her Doctorate in Education so that she can be in a position to help others believe in themselves and go far. At age 31, Dr. Alicia Holland opened a Not for Profit, Alise Spiritual Healing & Wellness Center and was officially ordained as a Minister. As a Transformational Life Coach, Professor, Author, Speaker, and Minister, Dr. Holland travels the World sharing her message: "You are Loved, You are Valued, and You are Competent.

Dr. Alicia Holland has two beautiful daughters, ages 7 and 9, who travels the World with her and are active participants in the Secret Sister Club Mentoring Program. She and her family resides in Austin, Texas and are currently looking for a new puppy.

Dr. Holland is available for speaking engagements and can be reached at support@thesecretsistersclub.com or support@iglobaleducation.com.

www.ingramcontent.com/pod-product-compliance
Lightning Source LLC
Chambersburg PA
CBHW071212130626
46555CB00004B/1674